MERARI'S
HOPE

MERARI'S HOPE

JENNIFER EUBANKS

Anomalos Publishing House
Crane

HighWay

A division of Anomalos Publishing House, Crane 65633

© 2008 by Jennifer Eubanks
Printed in the United States of America

08 1

ISBN-10: 0981495702 (paper)

EAN-13: 9780981495705 (paper)

Cover illustration and design by Steve Warner

A CIP catalog record for this book is available from the Library of Congress.

To Trevor, Leah, Tyler, Momma,
and Daddy, thanks for always believing in me.

A s THE SUN rose the cool crisp morning breeze blew through the arched window as father stormed into our bed chamber. "Girls, get up! I'm not going to tell you two again to get up and get ready to go to the market. Obed will be there waiting to deliver the produce and he will charge me extra if he has to wait. I'm not paying that low life any more than I have to for that second-rate produce he delivers."

I awoke to see father standing in the doorway with his hands on his hips in utter disgust that we were both not up and ready. "Father, if you dislike his produce then why do you buy it?" I asked sleepily as I rolled over and snuggled under the covers.

"Merari, why must you always question me? You should be thankful for the money the market brings in. If it wasn't for the money from the market you wouldn't be able to wear such elaborate clothing and take those trips you and your sister are always going on. You girls have no idea what it is to work. Just ask those peasant girls who beg in the streets what their lives are like. Why, you both would be up before me if you had to live like the other girls in this town."

As father droned on I noticed the morning mist as it rose and peeked over the windowsill. I loved the way it looked out our window early in the morning. The water bubbled up from the lush garden, creating a mist that intertwined with the sunlight. The sight was magical. It appeared as if thousands of diamonds were reflected sunlight in the garden like the twinkling stars in the night sky. I was jolted from my thought as my sister Mara plopped down on my bed.

Mara whispered, "Oh, yeah, right, there's no way we could ever be up before father. He sleeps with one eye open so no one will steal his money."

Mara didn't whisper quietly enough.

"You should be thankful I sleep with one eye open!" father bellowed. "When you come strolling in during the dark of night with your boyfriend of the week. I have to watch that he doesn't steal my money or valuables."

When father finished scolding Mara, mother quietly entered our bed chamber. "Girls, do as your father asks and give him no more grief, especially you, Mara," mother said. I watched mother for a few moments while father and Mara continued to argue. Even though her hair has highlights of grey it is no wonder that father was attracted to her at first sight. Father used to say her hair was "as black as night and her eyes as blue as the ocean". She is so petite it is no wonder she almost died giving birth. Father has always said she may be little but she has the will of a mad bull. Mara and I have never heard mother even raise her voice so we don't believe father about mother's strong will. Mara believes it is just one of father's crazy ideas. I sometimes think father is over protective of us because we both look so much like mother. Everyone in town says it is hard to believe sisters could look so much alike and not be twins. It is hard to believe that Mara is two years older than me by the way she carries on about everything.

"Merari! Stop day dreaming and get ready," father ordered. He stormed out so we could change. We heard him fussing at every servant as he went down the hallway, down the winding staircase, out the back door and to the barn to get the wagon.

I dragged myself out of the bed and dressed. Mara finally decided on which new dress to wear and rushed down stairs. Father was waiting for us in the wagon. We hopped in and he quickly snapped the horses and we were on our way. I could tell he was angry with us because he was muttering to himself. My mind wandered off as I observed the landscape on the way to the market. It was absolutely beautiful. The water quietly bubbled from the ground. The flowers were in full bloom and their fragrance was a sweet perfume in the morning air. The birds sang and I heard the large ones calling to their babies in the marshlands.

We reached the market just as Obed unloaded the first bushel of figs. It would have been a tumultuous ride if the landscape had not been so breath-taking because Mara and father argued the entire ride into town. I watched as father jumped out of the wagon to check that Obed was correctly unloading the figs. The market had the same smell as it did every morning. The combination of horses, fruit, and last night's liquor that was poured in the street or found its way into the street by more grotesque ways is not an aroma one appreciates but learns to endure. I have never understood why father always makes us go to market with him. It's uncommon for wealthy young women to be in the market place but father said it makes us appreciate what we have and all that he works for.

"Merari, what are you day dreaming about?" Mara squealed as she hurried over. "I have been trying to get your attention because here comes that new man I was telling you about. How are you ever going to find a man day dreaming?"

"Mara, I don't have to find a man."

"What do you mean?" Mara snapped. "Surely you aren't planning to live with mom and dad for the rest of your life."

"Why would I need to look for a man when you are always pointing out every man you see under the age of 125?"

"Ha, Ha! You think you're so funny. When was the last time you had a date, Ms. High and Mighty?"

"For your information, Ms. Mara-about-town, I've been seeing Japheth, Noah's son. If you would come home at night before the town gates are locked you would know that." I knew that would get her where it hurt. Mara hated to be the last to know about any romance or any other gossip.

"I have to listen to father lecture about my late night escaped but I don't have to hear it from you. Besides, why are you seeing that Japheth boy? He wouldn't know a good time if it hit him between the eyes. He and his brothers are so dull. They never come to any parties or any happening place. All they do is work, obey that invisible god, and listen to their crazy father. I mean, who ever heard of praying to a god that you can't see? And let's not forget that stupid boat they're building. I mean the whole family has to be a little crazy to spend all that time building a boat for water that is going to fall from the sky. Come on, Merari, don't you think you could find someone who's not quite so strange?"

"Mara, what are you talking about?"

"You know that thing they pray to that you can't see? Everyone else in this town prays to a god you can see. Most of the people I know pray to gods made of gold, silver, or jewels. Japheth and his family also believe that their god talks to Noah and no one else. What makes Noah so special? If this god is so great then why doesn't he speak to everyone? And if he was going to destroy the earth don't you think more than one person would know about it? Come on, sister, give me a break."

"So you would think Japheth and his family were not crazy if they did like father who prays to his money and fame," I said sarcastically.

"Merari, you can be so funny sometimes. It's just a waste to see that Japheth boy. You should sneak out with me and meet some real men."

"I don't think I could handle your men. I can't even keep up with who you are seeing. And you should not be so judgmental of Japheth and his family. At least they live what they believe and not just whatever philosophy or religion is popular at the moment. Actually I think there might be some value to what they say about their god." Mara looked at me like I was crazy and I am sure she was about to respond but father was yelling again.

"Girls, get over here!" Father was weighing the figs Obed had just unloaded and weighed.

"I guess we better help father before he throws a fit. You know, Mara, I think Obed has a crush on you." I jumped out of Mara's reach and ran to father before she could punch me. Obed has been in love with Mara since we were children. She pays no attention to him because he is beneath her, or so she says.

"Hi, Mara." Obed shyly smiled at her.

"Oh, hi, Obed," Mara said flippantly as she spotted her new conquest coming into the market.

Mara quickly scampered off to catch the attention of the new man. I was stuck listening to father and Obed quarrel about the price of figs per bushel.

2

A S OBED UNLOADED the last crate of figs a commotion stirred at the town gates. Father, Obed, and I paid no attention because there was always some kind of commotion in the market. Usually it was a scuffle or fight over the price of produce or someone stealing from a vendor. Father was finishing up his argument with Obed when I noticed the commotion coming toward us. I looked up and my mother's maid ran straight for us. It appeared she had run the entire way into town because her skirt was covered in dust; her face was red as fire and beads of sweat dripped from every pore. As soon as she saw me she burst into tears and began yelling, "You must come! You must come!"

I quickly ran to her and tried to console her. I could not calm her and all she would scream was, "You must come. You must come!" I glanced at father. He appeared concerned but did not ask what was wrong. He motioned for me to go with the maid back to the house. I had hoped he would come with us, but as I turned to leave the market I noticed why he did not want to leave. Edish, the most prestigious man in town, was headed directly toward father and Obed. Father had been hoping Edish would do business with him because of Edish's great fortune.

"Hurry! Hurry!" the maid screamed.

We ran like rabbits back to the house. When we reached the house the maid threw open the door and went up the stairs two at a time. I still had no idea what was wrong but when I realized where we were headed a frightening thought came over me. We were on our way to mother's room.

The last seven steps down the hallway were torturous. My feet felt as if they were running on desert sand that was slipping from underneath them. As we reached the door I saw the healer kneeling next to mother's bed. I had to stop and catch my breath before I entered. The room was so quiet my heavy breathing sounded like thunder in the room. I entered the room and almost fainted when I saw mother. She lay there lifeless and pale. It was hard to see the difference between her skin and the white fine linen sheets she loved. Her dark hair looked unnatural because of the contrast of color with her skin. My thoughts raced with panic and fear. Before I could speak the healer came to me.

"Merari, please sit down," the healer whispered in his soft caring voice.

I have always remembered him as loving and kind. Not

once had I ever heard him talk above a whisper no matter the situation. I sat on the stool beside the bed as I listened.

"Merari, your mother slipped on the slate floor in the living area. She was reaching for your grandmother's book of drawing on the shelf when the stool she was standing on broke. She fell and hit the area right below her skull on the desk." He lowered his head and swallowed hard.

Before he could continue I blurted out, "Is there anything you can do?"

He slowly raised his head, looked into my eyes and shook his head. I didn't want to believe him but I knew he was telling the truth.

"What are we to do to help her?" I asked in a quivering voice. "I can't let her just die without doing something."

"Merari, all you can do at this point is talk to her and let her know that you love her. I wish there was something I could do but at this point but all we can do is hope. To be honest, I don't even think hope can help, but you can try."

"Please, send the maid to get father and Mara from the market," I said.

As the healer rose to leave the room mother noticed me. She smiled and whispered, "There's my baby. Merari, please come and sit by me."

I was afraid to move from the stool. I feared that if I moved too quickly mother would slip away.

Mother whispered again, "Please, come and let me touch your beautiful face and hair one last time. I used to love brushing your long silky black hair when you were a child. I know it is possibly the last time I'll be able to feel your hair, skin, and smell the smell of my baby girl. You know it's funny, I never believed women when they said you could smell your children. I just thought they were being silly. I would always want to say we are humans not dogs. Why should you smell your children? But when I held you and your sister for the first time I knew instantly what those women meant."

"Mother, why are you saying a thing like this? You act as if it is the last time you will be with me or see me. You're not going to die. You're my momma, you can't die!" I had tried so hard to be strong but I couldn't hold back the tears. I am not sure if the tears came from the reality that my mother was dying or if it was from fear of death I guess that no matter how old you are you are never ready to accept the reality that your parents will be sick and then one day die. The thought of her being snatched away from me by such a stupid accident was sickening.

Mother touched my face with two of her fingers and brushed away the tears. "Now you stop that and listen," she said with determination. She tried to sit up but she didn't have the strength. She slipped back down in the bed. "I need you to look at grandmother's book of drawings. In the diary is an explanation of why you must marry Japheth. I was reaching for it when I fell."

I tried to interrupt but could not.

Mother continued in a struggling voice, "In the diary is the story of and explanation of hope. You must marry Japheth. Through him you will find the hope yet to come." Mother gasped for air. She pressed her hand on her left temple. Again her chest heaved as she tried to gasp for another breath. Her face wrinkled and winced to show the extreme pain she was feeling. Instinctively she reached for my hand to protect me from the grief I was about to experience, as her chest heaved once more. She glanced at me as if to say good-bye, took in two short strained gasps and then she was gone.

"No!" I screamed.

The healer came rushing back into the room and he pushed me to the side of the room as he examined my dead mother. I could not believe that within two short minutes she was gone. My thoughts were interrupted when the healer opened the door.

He looked at me with red, swollen, sad eyes and said, "I'm so sorry. She is gone. There was nothing I could do. I tried everything I knew but the injuries she received were to extensive." He then held me as we sobbed in the hallway together.

Immediately my thoughts returned to father and Mara. I had sent mother's maid to get them but no one had returned from the market.

I pushed away from the healer and said, "Why are father and Mara not here yet? What's taking so long?" I had no sooner got the words out of my mouth when I heard Mara screaming.

Mara shouted, "Merari, Merari! What's wrong? What's wrong with mother? I saw mother's maid running frantically in the market."

I did not have say a word. Mara immediately knew mother was gone when she saw the sadness in my eyes and tear stains on my face. I grabbed her and we hugged for what seemed like an eternity. Not a word passed between us but I knew we were both feeling the loss of our mother. At the same moment we realized mother would no longer be there to sooth a broken heart, to listen to our problems, to care for us when we are sick, to reassure us when we are scared or insecure, and most of all never again to share the special love a mother has for her children. Our grieving was interrupted by father's voice coming from the front atrium. Mara and I looked in each other's eyes and both wondered how father would react to the news of mother's death.

3

"WHAT IS GOING on around here?" Father shouted. As he busted in through the back door. His ranting continued as Mara and I sat huddled outside mother's bedroom. "My wife's maid runs into the market place like a lunatic screaming and disrupting everything. I have seen drunks, prostitutes, and beggars make less of a scene. What's going on? Why is it so quiet in this house?" Father ranted at the top of his voice. We knew he was coming closer because his screaming became louder and louder. His voice stopped when he reached the stairway that was at the end of the hallway that leads to mother's room. Mara and I did not say a word to each other we just looked at each other and wondered why we no longer heard his voice.

The moments passed slowly as we waited for father to reach the top of the stairs. My mind raced with thoughts on what he must be thinking. Then my mind detoured on to the thoughts of how to explain to him what had happened to mother. It was as if he all ready knew of the horror that awaited him at the end of the hallway. The house was deadly silent except for father's footsteps on the marble staircase. When he reached the top of the stairway he called out in a shaky voice, "Mara, Merari, where are you two?"

I tried not to cry so I took in a deep breath as Mara squeezed my hand for courage.

"Father, we are at the end of the hallway." After I spoke I quietly cried again. I knew he was coming and soon he would know mother was dead. We waited in dread for him as he made his way toward mother's room.

As soon as father rounded the corner the anger and determination disappeared from his face. His eyes darted from side to side taking in the scene. He looked at the healer then back to me and Mara. As soon as he saw us he fell to his knees and screamed, "NOOOOO!" We ran to him, reached our arms around him, and held him tightly as he cried. His sobs were so strong it was as if I could feel the pain in his heart. His tears fell to the marble floor. After a few moments he raised his head, wiped his eyes and nose and looked directly at me.

His eyes showed sadness and grief unlike any I had ever seen before. He appeared like a small child questioning his mother as he said, "How did she die?"

I looked to Mara for encouragement before I told my father how his wife of so many wonderful years had died,

but Mara had the same look as father. Before I could sum-
mon the courage to speak, father placed his hand on my hair
and pushed it behind my ears. He then brushed his thumb
against my temple. I knew this was the only way he could
provide support to help me tell him the details of his wife
and our mother's death.

As the three of us sat huddled on the floor in the hallway I told father the events that had led to mother's death.
"The healer was with mother when I got to her. He said
that mother was in the living area. She was trying to get
grandmother's drawings from the shelf when the stool she
was standing on broke. She fell and hit the area right below
her skull on the desk." I had to pause for a moment because
the tears running down father's and Mara's faces were too
hard to bear. I took a deep breath. Recounting the death of
my mother step by step was not something I ever wanted to
do again. Father held me tightly as we cried again. I did not
see her leave but I heard Mara's footsteps and sobs as she
ran down the hallway and stairs away from us. Mara could
not handle the extreme sadness and grief. I knew she needed
to be alone for a while.

After what seemed like an eternity father stopped hugging
me, looked me in the face and said, "The funeral arrange-
ments must be made." He squeezed my hand as he walked
away looking for the housekeeper.

I was concerned about the look in father's eyes when he
turned to go. He no longer had the look of grief and sadness,

but a look of determination as if on a mission. I pondered
the look of father as I walked slowly down the hallway and
steps away from my dead mother's room. I needed to check
on Mara.

$\mathcal{T}$HE NEXT FEW days passed as if I were living in a nightmare. Father had the staff prepare mother's body, even though it was customary for family members to prepare the body. I offered to help prepare the body but father said it was beneath us to touch and deal with a dead person. It hurt me that he felt his wife and our mother was just a dead body but instead of dealing with the pain I decided it was his way of dealing with grief.

I had not seen Mara for days. I was beginning to worry but the night before the funeral I heard her slip back into her bed. I immediately ran to her to see where she had been. I didn't even need to ask how she was dealing with her grief because she reeked of wine.

"Where have you been for the last few days?" I demanded.

In a slurred voice Mara responded, "What's it to you? You don't care about me. All you care about is moping around here feeling so sad that mother is gone and worrying about when Japheth will come by."

"How dare you speak of mother that way. I have the right to mourn her just as you do." I could not believe my sister could be so cold and callous. I was still trying to deal with father's ambivalence toward mother's burial preparations and now Mara was acting like this. I was so mad as these thoughts ran through my head that I could not think of another word to say, but then Mara slurred something.

"You think just because you got to Mother first that she loved you best. I would have been here but I was out doing my duty to find a suitable husband. You know where I've been? I've been at Edish's house meeting his son. We're getting married."

I could not believe what Mara was saying but the smell of wine on her breath reminded me that she probably didn't know what she was saying. I decided to leave her alone and talk with her in the morning. I got up to leave her bed and she grabbed my hand.

"Merari, I love you. Please, don't be mad," she said as she passed out in her bed.

I decided to dismiss the conversation we had just had because Mara was so drunk. I could not believe the events that had happened in the last few days and decided to climb back into bed and hope things were better in the morning.

The next morning the house buzzed with activity while everyone rushed around preparing for mother's funeral. I dressed in the mourning clothes father had had made and went to wake Mara. I tapped Mara because I was not sure of the mood she would be in. I did not want an episode like the one last night. She awoke and smiled, a half smile through barely open eyes, her loving smile.

"Merari, I'm sorry for whatever I said last night. I knew today was going to be horrible and I didn't want to think about it last night. I'm sorry I worried you. Please forgive me, and can you get me something for my head? It's killing me."

"I forgive you but you better get dressed or father will be mad. Your dress is hanging on the rack in the closet. Hurry, and I will meet you downstairs." I ran downstairs to check on father and to ensure everything was being taken care of.

As I entered the kitchen I noticed father sitting on the cushion in the bay windows looking out into the flower garden. "Father," I whispered. He turned and reached for me. I ran to him. As he held me in his arms he rubbed my back and caressed my hair.

He pulled away from me and said, "Today is going to be a very difficult day. I'm burying the love of my life. I'm sorry if I treated you harshly for the past several days but I just don't know how I'm going to live without her." His eyes filled with tears as he continued. "We've been together for so long and have experienced so much. You have no idea what she gave up to be with me." He stopped speaking as Mara entered the room.

19

"Hi, father. Are you two ready to go? Obed is at the front door to take us to town. He said the funeral procession will start at the front gates of town and we need to get going," Mara said.

Father looked crossly at Mara as he grabbed my hand. We all left the kitchen without saying a word. We reached the front gates of the town and were instructed by the security officers that we were to ride in the black carriage behind the white carriage carrying mother. I was surprised to see all of the people gathering along side the road to watch the processional. I glanced at Mara and noticed that she was already eyeing a boy coming in the gates.

"Mara, I can't believe you," I whispered.

"What are you talking about? I'm not doing anything wrong. I'm just watching that boy come through the gates."

I could not believe her attitude. "Would you please show some respect for mother? We are sitting behind her coffin and on our way to bury her. I can't believe you're thinking about boys right now," I said to her through clenched teeth.

"Girls, be quiet," Father said in a stern voice as he glared at us.

I just glared at Mara and gritted my teeth. Father turned back around just as the carriage lurched forward. We rode through town in silence. It was almost unbearable. The only sounds were the click clack of the horses' hooves and the creaking of the carriage wheels. Thousands of people lined the streets with their heads hung low as we passed. It was hard to believe the silence of sadness in the market place. Usually at this time of day it roared with activity. As the carriage rounded the corner I turned to look back. I gasped when I saw that everyone who was standing on the side of the streets had moved in the streets to honor mother. I cried thinking about the wonderful person who was in the coffin.

We reached the burial place that father had chosen. It was mother's favorite place in the countryside. She loved how the water sounded as it bubbled up from the ground and ran down the side of the sloping hill in a curvy pattern. She loved the view of the beautiful trees and flowers. If the wind blew in the right direction, she said you could smell the flowers on the hillside. It was a bittersweet memory as they slowly lowered her coffin in the ground. No words were spoken as we stood there and watched as the workmen shoveled dirt over our mother's casket. Father just stood there balancing on one foot and then the other. Mara and I stood holding each other and sobbing. Time seemed to stop during those dreadful moments.

Father motioned for us to get back in the carriage. When we got in the carriage he said quietly to us, "We'll go home. I think your mother would like to be alone in her favorite place. We'll come and visit tomorrow." The ride back to the house was quiet. The only sound was the click clack of the horses' hooves and the creak of the carriage wheels.

When we arrived home the carriage master took the carriage and we all walked quietly back into the house. Father went directly to his sitting room, Mara went to our room, and I was not sure what to do or where to go. As I wandered from room to room I passed by the room where mother had fallen. I slowly walked back to the room and stared at the closed door. Then I timidly placed my hand on the knob, but I was not sure why I was afraid to go in. Was it the fear of reliving my mother's final moments of health, facing the memories of a lifetime with my mother, or the dealing with the realization that my mother was gone? I slowly turned the knob and pushed open the door.

I gasped as I looked in the room. It had not been cleaned or straightened from the accident. The broken stool lay shattered on the floor. The desk on which mother had hit her head was in the same place except for a few items strewn on the top of it. I remembered Mother's last words. What did she mean by the "Hope yet to come"? My mind struggled to understand why the words were so important and why she said I must marry Japheth. I cried again, overwhelmed by my thoughts and emotions. As I raised my head from my hands and wiped away my tears, my emotions turned from confusion to anger. As I looked around the room I could not believe that the place of the accident, that lead to my mother's death could look so simple. Only a few objects were out of place but yet my life was in shambles. I dropped my head back into my hands and cried again.

"Merari, Merari! What are you doing in here?" father screamed from the door of the room.

I was jerked from my thoughts by his voice. As I wiped away the tears and tried to wipe my nose I could only muster a quivering quite voice to respond.

"I came in here to see where mother fell. I just had to see it." I was afraid my response was too honest because father had a vile and angry look on his face.

"How did you get in here? This door was to be locked and no one was to ever come in this room again. Merari!" he shouted, "I asked you, how did you get in this room?"

Father stood by the sofa. His large frame and angry face loomed over me. I answered in a shaky voice, "I just turned the knob." It was hard to speak because of my sobs.

"Get out of this room now!" Father yanked my arm and dragged me to the door. "You are never to come in here again! Also, you better not ask any questions about your grandmother's beliefs. I told your mother years ago all those words were stupid and nothing but garbage. They're only full of tales, fantasy, and crazy ideas." His eyes then filled with tears. "But did she listen? No! Your mother disobeyed me. She believed all that nonsense just like her mother did and look what happened to her. She's dead! Dead! Did you hear me? My love, my life, what I lived for is dead!" Father then slammed the door and stomped down the hallway.

I lay in the floor stunned and terrified at what had just happened. I could not believe how my father had just treated me. He had raised his voice several times but never had I heard him speak with such anger and hate. I had also never seen him lay a hand on Mara or me and for him to jerk me up from the sofa, drag me through the room, and throw me to the floor in front of the door. Again my mind was reeling from all that had just happened. I just couldn't comprehend the events of the day. In a time span of a few hours I witnessed the burial of my mother and saw a violent side of my father. I scraped myself off the floor and ran quickly outside to take a walk to collect my thoughts and for some fresh air. Maybe that would help ease my mind from the turmoil of the day.

5

A FEW DAYS PASSED and life slowly regained its daily routine. Father went to market every morning but Mara and I were no longer required to go. Mara slept late every morning because she would not come home until the wee hours in the morning. I never asked her where she had been anymore because it was useless. Her response, every time I asked was, "Why do you care? You just hang out with boring Japheth." It saddened me that our relationship was deteriorating. I did not understand why she had become so distant from me so all I could do was hope the relationship would change in the future.

My days were spent making sure the staff carried out the household duties correctly. I did not want another episode with father so I made sure everything was in its place. Because my mornings were busy, the afternoon became my favorite time of the day. After I finished my morning duties

I would sneak off to where Japheth and his family spent their days. I loved watching the building of the large boat even though I did not understand why it was so important to Japheth's family. I also enjoyed the company of Japheth's mother and two sisters-in-law. It was comforting to talk and laugh with other women since I no longer talked and laughed with Mara or my mother.

The tenth day after mother died, I awoke when Mara came dragging in just before the sun rose. I knew there was no hope of sleep so I got up to start my day. I dressed and went downstairs for breakfast and was surprised to see father sitting at the breakfast table. Usually he was gone by the time I started my day.

"Good morning, Merari," he said in his familiar loving voice. "You're up early. Any special plans today?"

"No, I just woke up and could not go back to sleep so I decided to start the day." I was glad that father appeared to be back to his old self. I had missed our talks and his company. I was going to keep the conversation light to avoid any outburst. I felt like I walked on eggshells through the house instead of marble and tile.

"Did Mara come in late again?" he asked sternly.

So much for keeping the conversation light. I was not sure how to answer but I knew to tell him the truth. "Yes," I said.

"I thought she had been staying out late but was not sure until yesterday. Yesterday, in the market, I was talking with Edish. You did know that we're business partners now, didn't you?"

I was surprised father had not told me about Edish because father was so determined to go into business with him. I knew Edish was extremely wealthy and that it was an excellent business maneuver on father's part.

"I didn't know that you two had joined forces. I knew that you were wanting to but did not know that it had happened," I responded.

"Yes, the deal was sealed only a few days ago and it's been a bit hectic working out all the details but I think it was an excellent business move. But now let me finish telling you about Mara. Edish said that Mara has been seeing his son. Apparently Cainon, Edish's son, is smitten with Mara. Edish believes there might be news of a wedding soon."

I, of course, did not tell father what Mara had told me in her drunken stupor about getting married so I acted innocent to see what else father would tell me. "Did Edish say anything else about Cainon and Mara?"

"No, that was about it. We joked about how perfect it would be if they married because then our families could be the wealthiest in this part of the world." Father laughed and shook his head as he drank the last sip of his juice. "Well, my child, I have to get to the market. I'll see you this evening." Father rose from his chair, kissed me on top of the head, and headed out the back door where the carriage was waiting.

I heard the back door shut and I breathed a sigh of relief. It appeared father was back to his old self, but I was surprised about the news of Mara's potential marriage. When she had told me I thought it was the alcohol or her hopes talking. I never believed it to be true. It suited her perfectly to marry a rich man who could give her everything she could want and to receive father's blessing. I knew I had to tell Japheth of the news and it could not wait until the afternoon. I ran and found the head housekeeper to give her the instructions of what needed to be done. As soon as I finished speaking with her I ran quickly to where Japheth and his family worked.

I was completely out of breath when I reached to edge of the clearing where I knew Japheth, his two brothers, their wives, and his father and mother would be. As I stooped down to catch my breath, I felt the earth tremble beneath my feet. I quickly grabbed on to a nearby oak tree because I thought I was in an earthquake. As I held on to the tree the trembling ground turned to shaking ground. I held on tighter to the tree hoping the deep roots of the tree would not shake loose. The shaking increased and when I looked down I saw bits of grass and dirt shake loose from the ground. I realized that this was not an earthquake because too much time had passed. Earthquakes only lasted a few short minutes and it felt at least five had passed. The intensity of the shaking increased so I held tighter to the tree. I was holding on so tightly that the bark dug into the side of my cheek. Suddenly my feet slipped and I slid down the side of the tree. As I slid down the tree I felt the bark cutting into my hands, arms and face. I lay there hoping that whatever this was would end soon and that the deep roots of the tree would not shake loose. Then I heard a sound I had never heard before coming from behind me. At first I could not see anything over the rise of the hill because the sun was blinding me with its fiery pink morning rays. I could not place my hand over my eyes to shield the sun but suddenly enormous shadows fell on the hillside. The sound became louder, louder, and louder. At first I was terrified because the sound reminded me of when the large, scaly, man-eating animals came to our village when I was a child. I wanted to let go of the tree and run but I knew I couldn't. If the man-eating animals caught scent of the blood trickling down my face, I could not outrun them, so I lay there for what seemed like hours. Then as suddenly as the trembling began it stopped. The sound also stopped. Although frozen by fear, I slowly lifted and turned my head to see if I could see what caused all of the commotion. As my eyes scanned the surrounding area I saw shadows over the hillside. I was not sure to trust my eyes, but I saw all shapes and sizes of shadows.

"Merari! Are you all right?" Japheth shouted.

I saw Japheth running toward me. I knew I looked a mess because of the terrified look on his face. He grabbed me and held me tight.

"Oh, my goodness! What happened? Are you all right?" Japheth's voice was filled with terror and concern.

"I think so." I knew I looked a mess because of the fresh dirt that was unearthed during the commotion was covering my dress and the blood trickling down my face and hands. I brushed the dirt from my skirt as Japheth used a rag to wipe the blood from my face. His large hands gently wiped the blood.

"Merari, I want you tell me everything that happened here," Japheth said.

We sat down on the fresh soil that had been unearthed. I was no longer concerned about my skirt getting dirty because it was already covered with dirt and with drops of blood. I slowly told Japheth of everything that had happened. He sat in awe as I spoke. I shook as I explained every detail. To comfort me, Japheth wrapped his strong arms around me. I was only halfway through my story when Japheth stopped me.

"Merari, let's go back to my house. You're trembling like the ground that you describe. Mother will give you some water and something to put on your cut. You can also lie down for a while then you can finish telling your story."

Japheth helped me to my feet and securely held my hand as we walked back to his home. As we walked back in silence I noticed we were taking a different route back to his home.

"Japheth, are we going to your home? I've never been this way before."

"I decided to take a shorter path."

I had no reason to doubt Japheth, but he had a funny look on his face. I did not question him because after the day I had experienced anything was possible.

6

WHEN WE ARRIVED at the site of the ark we found chaos. Japheth's two brothers, Shem and Hem, and his father Noah were scurrying in and out of the ark with loads of hay, feed, and grain. Neither Japheth's mother nor his two sisters-in-law were in sight. Noah finally saw us standing there watching the commotion and waved.

"Hello, you two!" He walked toward us.

I must have looked a fearful sight because when he was close enough to see us he paused and then ran toward us.

"Merari, what has happened to you? We must get you back home for mother to help clean you up."

Noah looked quizzically at Japheth as to search for an answer but then it was as if Noah instantly knew what had happened. They shared a quick quirky smile as Noah shook his head and reached for my arm. I tried to protest and say that I was fine but Noah quickly took charge of the situation. He grabbed my arm and pulled me toward the house.

"Japheth, go tell your brothers, Shem and Ham to make sure the animals are secure and then meet us back at the house. It's almost time for lunch and your mother will be waiting. I'll go ahead with Merari and you three come as soon as you finish."

"Yes, sir. We'll hurry so we don't keep mother waiting," Japheth replied.

Before I could walk away Japheth kissed me on the forehead. Noah walked me to the house. I tried to explain the reason for my injuries and to tell of my experience but Noah would not listen.

"You hush now. I know you've had an eventful morning. That sure is a nasty scrape on your face but mother will clean you up, don't you worry," Noah said in a hurried tone.

I had no doubt that Japheth's mother would care for my wounds but I wanted to tell Noah about what I had experienced. I soon realized he had no concern of my experience because he kept talking about what he wanted for lunch. I started to ask about the progress of the ark and how soon he thought it would be finished but we reached Japheth's home before I could ask. We reached the gate of the front walkway when Japheth's mother saw us.

"Merari, what happened to you? Come in my dear and let's clean you up. That's a nasty scrape and we need to get all of the dirt and blood off your face and hands. How in the world did this happen?" Japheth's mother asked frantically.

I tried to start to explain but she interrupted me.

"Hush, girl. Be real still and quiet while I wash your face and clean you up. Here hold this rag on your cheek while I go and get something to put on your cuts."

I sat quietly and waited for her to return. Japheth's mother was an immaculate housekeeper. Today the house seemed disheveled. There were clean clothes stacked neatly in piles but they were not put away. Also I had not seen Shem and Hem's wives. I was jerked from my thoughts as Japheth's mother reentered the room with a jar of something and a white bandage in her hand.

"Hold still while I put this on your face. It will sting for a minute but then you will feel a cool soothing sensation. I'm also going to place this bandage on your face".

I sat still while she bandaged my face. I had always found Japheth's mother to be an interesting woman. She was quiet, yet she had a side to her that I rarely saw in women. She would take charge if necessary, freely share her opinion, and she never missed a chance to tell a joke or pull a joke on anyone. I was intrigued by her because she was so different from my mother.

"There you go. All cleaned up. Now come in the kitchen and tell me how this happened."

"Mother, the boys are back and so are the other girls. I

think we need to eat lunch so we can get back to the ark," Noah interrupted.

"Oh, all right then. Come on and tell everyone to sit down. I'll put lunch on the table and we can eat. You're right, Noah, we need to hurry because it appears the time is nearing."

I was confused about their conversation and wanted to ask what they were talking about but I did not want to appear rude. So I offered to help.

"I'll be glad to help you with the food," I said.

"No, no, no. You go sit right next to Jahpeth and rest. You've had an exhausting day. I'll get the food. Go sit right over there. That's where Japheth sits," Japheth's mother said as she pointed to a chair over on the edge of the table.

"No need to argue with her, Merari. Just do what she says and she'll take care of the rest," Noah said affectionately about his wife.

I started to sit down as Jahpeth, Shem and his wife, and Ham and his wife entered the kitchen.

"I see mother has taken care of you," Jahpeth said in a loving tone as he leaned over the washtub to scrub his hands.

I smiled at Japheth. I felt the flutter of excitement race through my blood. Every time he spoke in his loving voice and glanced at me I had the same feeling. "I offered to help her with the food but she would not hear of it. She told me to sit and rest before we eat."

Ham's wife grinned at me as she took her seat at the

table. "Merari, you'll learn not to argue with mother. She always gets her way so just do what she says. I learned the hard way when Ham and I were first married."

She giggled at Japheth's mother and Ham as she continued with the story. "The first week we were married I decided to have a dinner party for everyone at our house. Mother had asked what was for dinner and I explained it was a new dish that I had seen a traveler preparing in the market. I went on and on about how good the dish was and how I had bought a bag of the special seasoning from the traveler to make the dish just as he had prepared it. I had a tiny bit of the seasoning left in the bag and mother insisted on smelling the bag of seasoning. I wondered why she wanted to smell the bag of seasonings and she gave the excuse that she had smelled the smell before but couldn't quite name the smell."

I was confused at the story so I asked, "How could she smell the seasonings if she had not yet smelled the bag?"

"Oh, I am sorry I left out a part. Mother had smelled the dish simmering on the oven when she came in the house and was curious of the smell. So anyway I hand her the bag and she sticks her nose right over the opening and takes a big breath. The smell had not reached her nose when she threw down the spice bag, began coughing, her eyes watering and turning red. She was hooting with laughter at the same time. She created such a noise that Ham, Noah, Japheth, Shem, and his wife came running in the house. After she gained her composure she asked me, 'Lathea do you have any idea what's in the seasoning?' I told her I bought it from the traveler. 'Lathea that's nothing more that horse feed ground up with a little pepper and salt.' I was so embarrassed but everyone else thought it was hilarious. Needless to say we didn't eat the dish, but have had a great laugh about that story ever since."

"Merari, pay no attention to that girl," Japheth's mother said winking at Lathea. "She's full of all kinds of untrue tales about me. She makes me out to be a horrible mother-in-law who cares nothing about her." Japheth's mother then reached across the table and lovingly squeezed Lathea's hand.

I felt awkward as I watched the two exchange such a loving gesture. I was not sure if it was because I felt like an outsider who did not understand their relationship or if it was because I knew I would never share a moment like that with my mother. I was interrupted from my thoughts when Noah called my name.

"Merari? Why don't you tell us what happened to you today?" Noah said as he looked from me to the rest of the family sitting around the table.

"Well, sir, I was coming to see Japheth to tell him of the news my father had shared with me at breakfast this morning. He told me that me sister Mara might marry Cainon, Edish's son. Apparently father and Edish have gone into business together and that is how Cainon and Mara met. Father was simply delighted at the thought of the two marrying. I was quite shocked at the news and was on my way to tell Japheth when it all started." I was about to continue my tale when a ruckus arose outside the door.

Noah and the three boys jumped up from the table and ran to the door. Japheth's mother rushed the rest of us out of the kitchen and into the living room. The living room was quite small as all four of us huddled into the corner. I was about to ask Lathea what was going on but I then noticed the three ladies had their heads bowed and eyes closed. They whispered to themselves. I assumed they were praying to their invisible god. Not knowing what to do or say I just bowed my head and closed my eyes. As we sat there I heard the commotion outside and turned my attention to what was being said and to listen for any familiar voices.

The first voice I heard was Noah's. I heard him say, "What can we help you people with today and why have you come?"

The next voice was deep and as the man spoke his speech was filled with a tone of sarcasm and ridicule. The man said, "Noah, we heard a loud commotion out this way and knew only you and your family could create such a disturbance so we all decided to come out and see what was going on. We also did not hear the clanging, banging, and hammering of nails that we have heard for the last one hundred years from out this way. We thought maybe your God, who no one can see, had taken you all up to be with him or maybe your God had gotten fed up with all your stupid ideas and killed you off."

I heard a roar of laughter from what sounded like a large crowd. I then heard a few cheers and jeers from individuals but I did not recognize any of the voices. Apparently this man was the spokesman for the group because he spoke again.

"Noah, what you do you have here, a zoo? Why we have never seen all the kinds of animals you got out here and all along the hillside. What are you going to do with all of these animals? Do you mean to raise all these animals? We noticed you have a male and female of each kind. Why if you go into the breeding business you might make enough money and be as rich as our friend Cainon here." Laughter erupted from the crowd and this time with cheers of sarcastic comments.

Oh, no! My thoughts quickly raced to Mara. Cainon, surely that is not the man my sister is to marry? I abandoned my thoughts as I heard Noah begin to speak. Apparently Noah knew the spokesman of the group because he called him by name.

"Amoritus, I know you and your group are curious of my family's actions because for the past ninety-nine years you all have come to see and poke fun at my family, my family's faith, and our construction of the ark. However, I'm glad you came today with such a large group. Today's the day I'll tell you the most important words I have ever told you. You know that I have said that my God, who loves each one of you, is going to send a flood to destroy the entire earth. My God is going to destroy the earth because he is grieved at how humans have abandoned his teaching and no longer love and worship him. He knows that men are evil and He feels there is no other way but to destroy everything living on the earth. I have told you this day after day but yet no one has believed my words or remembered God because none of you have chosen to leave your wicked ways and turn back to the God who created you."

I was not surprised at Noah's message because I had heard it from the town's people, Mara, father, and even Japheth but I still did not understand and why today was more important than any other day. He was still saying the same thing he had been saying for almost one-hundred years.

"I know all of you are thinking, yeah, yeah, we have heard all this before, but today's the most important day of my message." Noah said, "Today God has shown us that His plan is about to be fulfilled."

I heard the spokesman interrupt Noah. "Sure, Noah, how do you know? Did your invisible god speak to you again?"

The crowd erupted with laughter. They quieted down as Noah spoke again.

"No, Amoritus. He sent a male and female of each type of animal to go into the ark with us. Surely, even you can believe this because you've seen it with your own eyes. That's why all of the commotion took place this morning. The animals were coming to get into the ark so they will be saved from the flood that's about to take place."

I heard Amoritus' voice again. "Noah, you expect us to

believe that your God sent all of these animals from all over the world so they can be saved on your boat? Why surely it's just some type of migration pattern or the animals were just annoyed at all the banging and came to tell you to shut-up." Again the crowd roared with laughter.

As I listened to Noah's argument, I realized what I had experienced today. It was the animals coming to the ark. I wanted to believe Noah but what he was saying was crazy so I strained my ears to hear more information about the ark and the animals.

"Amoritus," Noah began, "I had hoped that you and all of your friends would believe what I'm saying, but yet you still don't believe. Soon a time will come when you will want to believe but it will be too late. I beg you to please listen to the words I speak because they were sent from God to warn you about what's about to happen. All I can do is tell you what I know to be true and pray that you listen and believe. If you choose not to believe, that's your choice and you'll have to suffer the consequences of your decisions."

After hearing Noah's words I decided to believe in what he was saying even though I did not understand it. I am not sure why I believed him but as I looked around the crowded living room I could not doubt the faith of the three women around me. The dying wish of my mother entered my mind. There had to be something to what Noah was saying. Mother must have believed or she would not have told me to marry

Japheth. My thoughts were interrupted as I heard Amoritus' voice again.

"Noah, you expect us to believe that your god, whom no one can see or hear, is going to kill all of the humans but save a male and female of each kind of animal. Noah, you have been out in this hot sun for too long and your brain is fried. Only you and your stupid family believe this hog wash and we will sit back and laugh when nothing happens. Hey, you also expect us to believe that water is going to fall from the sky. You know good and well water doesn't fall from the sky. It comes up from the ground. Noah, your ideas are as stupid as your god. There's no way any intelligent person would believe your words! You're just a crazy old man!"

Apparently Amoritus was now addressing his group of friends because he said, "Come, ladies and gentlemen, let's leave this old coot and go worship our gods of wine, women, good time, and the greatest god of all, money. At least we get some satisfaction from them and our gods don't fill our heads with crazy ideas."

I heard shouts of laughter and hollering as the voices faded into the distance. I felt a hand on my shoulder so I raised my head and noticed Japheth's mother rising from her huddled position and walking toward the kitchen. As I stood Noah, Japheth, Shem, and Ham returned. We all gathered back into the kitchen to discuss what had just happened at the front door.

7

A S JAPHETH WALKED me back to my house my mind swirled with questions of what had happened and what I had been told was about to happen. It had been an overwhelming day with unbelievable events. Everything seemed to be happening so fast and the explanations that I had been given were too much for me to comprehend or believe.

"Japheth, it's so hard to believe what you are telling me. I want to believe but I'm struggling with all this. I can't understand how you talk of a God of love and caring when in just a few days he's going to destroy the whole world and everything in it except you, your family, and a few animals. What you say sounds crazy."

"I know, but you have to believe. It's what father calls faith and from what I've seen over the past one-hundred years, everything God has told father has come true. I struggle to believe it, too. I'm not my father. I don't have his undoubting faith and love of our God, but I trust and believe the best I can. Father says that's all that God requires."

"What do you mean all he requires?" I still did not understand all that Japheth was telling me and I hated to keep questioning but if I was to be his wife I had to know what I was about to get into.

Japheth slowly took a deep breath and held my hands as he explained the essence of his faith and understanding of his God. "Here, Merari, let's go sit under that tree and talk about this." We walked hand in hand then sat under a tree. Japheth then explained his God. "My God is a God of love, caring, and forgiveness. He always wants what's best for His people. I have seen this for myself and my ancestors were living proof of that love and forgiveness. I've heard stories all of my life about how God cared for them and provided for them even when they did not deserve it."

"What do you mean by 'even when they did not deserve it'? I've always believed the saying 'you get what you deserve' was true. I thought that's how things worked."

"Merari, think back to the story of Adam and Eve."

"You mean the old story of how we all got here on earth? Japheth, you know that can't be true. To believe that there was a perfect world, a talking snake, and that one decision changed the course of history and how we live. That's ridiculous! If God is a God of love then why did he kick them out of the garden and make their life so difficult? If He loved them so much why didn't he just forgive their mistake and let them go on about their business?"

"You see, if He didn't love them He would have said that. He had to show them what they did was wrong. Yes, God is a God of love, but He's also a just God and must do what's fair and right. If he didn't do what was fair and right, He wouldn't be God. If He had let them go on their way they would not have understood that disobeying God was wrong and that there are consequences for disobeying God. The consequence of their disobedience was to have a difficult life with problems and sorrow, but God—being a God of love—also provided for them outside of the garden. He gave them clothing, a food supply, and most importantly, hope."

"Hope? How can they have hope when they are going to have to work for their food, have pain, sorrow, and poor Eve and every other woman has to suffer in childbirth and other womanly ways? I don't see any hope in that." I was trying not to become aggravated at Japheth but all of this was so hard to believe. "Also, how could they have hope if in only a few generations God destroys everything again? Is it his plan to start all over again because his first plan didn't work?"

"I don't have all the answers and probably never will but all I can do is have faith and trust in the Hope that is to come."

In that instant my mind spun back to my dying mother's bedside. Japheth had just repeated the last words my mother had said to me. My mind swirled.

"Merari, are you all right? Your face is as white as a ghost. What's wrong?"

"Japheth, those were the last words my mother said before she died."

"What words, what are you talking about?" Japheth said confused.

"The Hope that is to come. Those are the last words my mother said before she died. She said that's why I had to marry you. Japheth, I need to go home and think about this. Remember, I love you and I'll see you tomorrow." I quickly kissed him on the cheek and turned and ran home. As I ran I heard Japheth calling for me but all I could think of were my mother's last words.

8

WHEN I RAN in the front gate my mind was whirling with all the news and events that had taken place. As I opened the front door the excitement in the front hallway was spinning more than the thoughts in my head. Mara stood in the middle of the room barking orders at the servants in her shrill voice. She glanced around as I closed the heavy door behind me. Mara grabbed me, swung me around, and started screaming, "It's happening, it's happening!"

"Is something wrong? What is all the excitement about?" I was so glad to see that she was back to her old self but I truly wondered what was going on.

"Cainon asked me to marry him. He's talked to father and everything. I'm going to be a bride, a beautiful bride, and a wealthy, wealthy bride. How much better could life be? You have to be my maid of honor. There's no question about it. I'll tell the dress maker to go ahead and make your gown when she makes mine. Oh, and I have to buy flowers. There's so much to do. Merari, stop standing there and get busy helping me."

"When is the wedding?" I asked. Mara was in such an uproar that I knew that the date had to be soon.

"Date what date? I don't have a date with Cainon. We're getting married not going on a date. What a stupid thing to ask."

"No, when is the date of the wedding?"

Mara laughed hysterically. "Oh, Merari, I'm so sorry. I'm in such a tizzy that I didn't even realize what you were asking me. We haven't set the date yet. All I know is that I'm getting married and there are things that need to be done. We talked about the date of the wedding but Cainon said he wanted to get married as soon as possible because he would soon have to take a trip and he needed to get the date set for the trip and then we could set the wedding date."

"So you don't know when you will get married or how soon?"

"Merari, are you not listening? I just told you," Mara said disgustedly.

I hated to tell her that it had to be soon or there would be no wedding because of what God was about to do. "Mara, you need to make your wedding as soon as possible because Japheth said..."

"I don't want to hear about that ridiculous boat, what your stupid boyfriend said, or what his crazy father is telling you. You have got to quit listening to those fools. People are going to think you believe as they do and then they might even think I believe in that hog wash. Now shut up and help me get this wedding together." Mara's voice rang out through the marble hallway.

"Mara, calm down I have to tell you something."

"What? It better not be about that stupid Japheth boy," Mara said.

"Japheth is not stupid." I said in a stern voice. "Now you shut up for a minute and listen to me. I'm going to marry Japheth tomorrow because God is about to carry out his plan. Don't roll your eyes at me. I know you don't believe any of this but you have to believe me. I don't understand it all either but God is going to destroy the whole earth and everything in it. If you don't believe you can't go into the ark and you'll die. Mara, please listen to me. I love you and I want you to go with us." I didn't get to finish talking to her because she spun around, turned her back on me and walked back toward the kitchen shaking her head.

All I heard her say was "You have lost your mind and I don't have time to listen to that hog wash."

As I stood in the hallway of my beautiful home my heart was breaking. I knew what I had experienced today and what I had heard Noah say. I wanted to believe Noah and Japheth, but Cainon and his friends had a point, too. I mean it had been one hundred years since Noah began saying what God was going to do and nothing had happened yet. But then, why did all the animals show up? Then Japheth talked about Hope to come and that was the last thing mother had said. I was so confused except for one thing. That one thing was that I loved Japheth and I planned to marry him. So what if this God thing didn't work out? We would be together. I knew I had to tell father my news. He would think I was crazy just as my sister had. I was about to lose my sister, my father, my beautiful home, and everything that I had known all of my life for the love of a man, the love of a God, and for a Hope that was yet to come. As I trudged up the stairway to my room I wondered if maybe Mara was right. I just might be crazy.

9

I AWOKE TO THE sound of Mara rustling through her closet. Through sleepy eyes I watched her throwing things on to the floor. She mumbled to herself. I rose up and propped myself on my elbows. After a long yawn I asked her what she was doing.

"Good morning, sleepy head," Mara said teasing.

I was glad to see that her mood toward me had changed. "What are you doing and why are you throwing all of your beautiful clothes on to the floor?"

"I'm having an engagement party tonight and I have to find something to wear," Mara said as she continued to throw clothes onto the floor.

"An engagement party? Tonight? What's the rush?" I couldn't understand why the party was tonight. She had just told me that she was to be married. Usually it takes months to plan a wedding and all the parties.

Mara looked at me disgustedly. "Why are you asking me all of these questions? If you are so concerned then get up and help me find something and, by the way, you need to find something, too."

"Mara, you still didn't answer my question. What's the rush?"

"Cainon has a business trip across the sea and he wants me to go with him. He says that it would not be proper for me to go with him if we were not married. He thinks we'll be gone for at least a month or so."

"Mara, don't take this the wrong way but why are you worried about if it would look proper? That has never stopped you before. And I don't think anyone would really care," I said somewhat teasingly toward Mara.

"I'll tell you why I'm going. I just hate to have to wait for him to get back. He said it could be a month or maybe longer. Now how would it look if I get engaged and my finance runs off for months before our wedding? I mean all the other girls would think it was an arranged marriage just for position."

I slyly grinned at Mara and asked, "Could those other girls be wrong?"

Mara looked at me in anger. "All right, Mrs. high and mighty. There may be some truth to that but I couldn't pass up the opportunity to marry one of the richest men in the world could I? Just think of all of the wonderful things I'll have being married to him. I mean money, jewels, clothes, homes, travel, and anything my heart desires."

"Do you really love him?" I asked. I knew my question cut Mara to her heart because she turned back to her closet.

I had a hard time hearing her through the rustling of her dresses but I faintly heard her say, "Well, you can marry that silly Japheth boy for love if you want but I know what I want and what's important in life."

I started to respond but father's voice rang out from our bedroom door. "Good morning, girls. Mara, have you found a dress yet?"

As soon as I heard his voice I remembered the news I had to tell him and my stomach and heart seemed to intertwine within my chest.

"Good morning, Merari," father said.

"Good morning, father." I quickly looked away.

Gently grabbing my elbow, father asked, "Merari, is there something wrong? Your eyes seem troubled."

Before I could think I blurted out, "I need to talk to you about something." I couldn't believe the words had just jumped of my mouth. It was as if someone else spoke for me.

"Is there something wrong?" father responded.

"We just need to talk and in private." I got out of bed threw on my robe and led father down the hallway, down the steps, and to the kitchen.

"Merari, what is wrong and why couldn't you talk in front of your sister? Are you upset about her sudden marriage?" father questioned me as we walked toward the kitchen.

When we reached the kitchen I asked father to sit down. I didn't know how he would respond thinking back to his reaction when mother died. I did not want him to feel abandoned because both Mara and I had plans to leave. We sat down at the table as I tried to muster up the courage to tell my news.

"I am not sure how to tell you this. I mean it's not like I don't want to or that I am afraid of my decision or…"

"Merari, what are you talking about? It possibly can't be that bad. I guess I can't even understand what you're saying."

I took a deep breath, found my courage and blurted out, "I'm going to marry Japheth and it has to be done today." After the words had slipped out I felt a huge relief and the knots and tightness in my chest were relieved. I anxiously awaited the lashing from father, but as I looked at him from across the table I was surprised by the look on his face.

His eyes began to fill with tears and the tears looked as if they were about to burst over like the edge of a rushing river. His bottom lip quivering, he bit it with his two front teeth. He grabbed my hands and vigorously rubbed his thumbs over my hands. I was utterly speechless because this was not the reaction I expected from him. He took a deep breath, slowly exhaled, and spoke.

"Merari, I knew this day would come. I knew that Japheth was the one you would marry. I knew the day you told me what your mother had said. I'm sorry for the way I reacted that day. It's just..." Father stopped and wiped away a few of the tears that rolled down his face. "It's just that your mother believed in Noah and I didn't. I knew when you started hanging around with Japheth that you would love him and believe in his God."

"Father, what are you talking about? You knew mother believed in Noah and you didn't? I don't understand." I had never seen this side of my father before.

"Merari, you know that Noah has been preaching about God's punishment on man for years. Of course, everyone has heard it. It's just that your mother believed in Noah. She believed in all of the old stories of God and what he could do and what He has promised that will come. I don't believe. I'm a man who believes in what's real, what I can see and taste and feel. I don't have time to believe in hopes and dreams and things I cannot see. And as a matter of fact I've done pretty well for myself. I was a good husband and have always tried to be a good father to you and your sister. I'm not perfect. I don't pretend that I am." As he spoke, tears flowed freely down his face.

I was not expecting this reaction at all from father. I sat there for a moment not knowing what to do or say. So I reached out to father and tightly held his hands. "You were a good husband to mother and everyone knew you loved her very much and you have always been a wonderful and loving father to me and Mara. No one can doubt that. I just don't understand how mother could believe one thing and you another. She never told us or led us to believe that you two disagreed on anything. Aren't you scared that maybe what Noah is saying is true?"

"Merari, first of all, your mother was a good woman and many years ago we both agreed that she could believe in her God and I in mine. It just happened to be that my god is one of money, supporting one's family, and work. I know your mother respected that but she never once stopped trying to get me to believe in her God. Your mother not only loved her God but she loved me and accepted me for me and not what I was or wasn't. I'm not sure if that was good or bad but that's the way it was. It worked for us. The one thing I'm sure of is that every man will die and maybe my way to die is to drown in water coming down from the sky. I will accept my fate and hope for the best."

I could not believe my ears. I had no idea that father and mother had ever had any type of conversation or understanding toward each other on their beliefs. They had never mentioned their faith or what either one believed about God or spiritual matters. I was glad that father and had told me his true feelings because we had never had such a wonderful conversation. It was nice to finally understand the man I had loved and admired for so many years and to understand why mother had said those words to me. I couldn't believe that she, too, believed in Noah and God's plan. Maybe what Noah said was true. At that very moment I knew I was doing the right thing. Even thought I didn't understand everything, I believed in Japheth and what he said about his God.

Father rose from the table, pulled me close to him, and hugged me until I thought I was going to break in half. After a few moments he took a step back and lovingly looked at me and said, "Now, Merari, you're doing the right thing. It's obvious you love Japheth so follow our heart. I hate to lose you but it's easier for me because I know your mother would have been ecstatic. She would have approved of your marriage to Japheth and the acceptance of his God. I wish I could have given your mother that but I just couldn't make myself believe in her, Japheth's, Noah's and now your God. I know you will be happy and that's all a father could ever want for his baby girl. Well, you need to go tell your sister the good news because you have a lot to do if you're going to be married tonight. You run on upstairs and tell your sister and I'll get the servants to pack your things."

I hugged father again. I could not believe he approved of my marriage to Japheth. I ran upstairs to tell Mara the news. When I got to our room I found Mara's maid hanging up the dresses Mara had thrown on the floor.

"Where is Mara?" I asked.

"She said she had to go down to the vault to decide on what jewels to wear with the gown she had chosen," the maid responded.

I don't know how I missed her coming down the steps

as I was going up, unless she went down the back stair case. If she had gone down the back she could have gotten to the vault quicker and there wasn't much time to waste. Father interrupted my thoughts.

"Where is Mara? I thought she was here," father said as he stepped into the room.

"Apparently she went down to the vault to get jewels to wear to her party. I can't believe that girl. I have to go and I won't have a chance to see her. Father, why did she run away?" I said as I sobbed.

Father hugged me.

"Merari, don't worry. I'll find her and tell her to see you at Japheth's. I'll tell her why you had to go and the reasons you left in a hurry. Now let me walk you down and out of the house. I won't be at your wedding but I can walk with my baby girl down the steps and out the front door with my blessings," father said in a loving voice.

When we reached the front door father handed me the bag that had been packed for me. I could not believe that it was time for me to leave my wonderful home. In only a few short hours my life would change as I became Japheth's wife.

"Merari, don't look so sad," father said with a smile. "You're about to be married to the man you love and in your heart you know this is the right decision." Father stroked my face as he said these loving words.

"I'm very happy. I just hate to leave in such a hurry. I

didn't even get to tell Mara goodbye. I know this is the right thing because I feel it in my heart and I love Japheth very much. It makes it easier to leave knowing that you understand and that mother told me to marry him." As I said the words I knew I was making the right decision to leave and marry Japheth even though many people would not understand why I was marrying him.

"Merari, my love, you need to go or Japheth is going to think you have changed your mind," father said as he grabbed me and held me as tight as he could for a long time. "Go. I know you'll be a beautiful bride. Tell Japheth that he is a very lucky, lucky man. And you know you can always change your mind and come back home."

"I know father. I love you very much. I love you and I'll talk to you soon." As the last words I said trickled out of my mouth I had a strange feeling. It was almost as if I knew I would never be back. I quickly dismissed the thought because I had to see Mara one more time before she left for her trip.

I gave father one last giant hug, grabbed my bag, and turned around to head to Japheth's home. As I turned around with my back to father and my old life and I faced my new life. I felt a peace and confidence in my decision. At that moment all my fears and doubts fell away. I knew that I had made the right decision to believe in Japheth, Noah, and their God. I walked toward my new life, the life that was waiting for me. As I continued to walk away I felt a pull in my heart toward Japheth's home. It was as if I was being drawn by some strange force toward him and the life that was promised with him. As I walked farther from my home I had no desire to look back even though father was probably still standing by the door watching me leave. Suddenly, a desire to begin my new life with Japheth overtook me and it was as if my feet could not move fast enough. I ran to my new life and the hope my new life promised.

10

MY MIND BUZZED with all of the thoughts of what my life would be like with Japheth when I heard his voice calling to me. Japheth ran toward me and he appeared to be in quite a panic.

He stopped in front of me and had to lean over and prop himself up on his knees to catch his breath. His hair, dripping in sweat, fell down over his brow. I could not see his face or understand what he was saying through his huffing and puffing.

"Japheth, what's the matter? Why are you in such a hurry? Take a breath and tell me what is wrong."

"There is no time," Japheth wheezed.

"No time? No time for what?"

"We have to go into the ark now. God told father that the time has come."

"Why can't we wait a few days? I have to go see Mara and

tell her about our wedding and find out all about her wedding. I can't go now I have to much left to do. I have to say good-bye to my sister," I said. Panic squeezed my throat.

"We can talk about this on the way back to the house. I have to help get the rest of the things loaded into the ark," Japheth said.

He grabbed my hand and pulled me as we ran back to the ark. I was having a hard time keeping up with him because the way Japheth was carrying my bag and dragging my hand the bag kept bumping me in the leg and I had a hard time trying to keep from falling. I finally had enough and pulled my hand away from Japheth's grip.

"Japheth, stop and tell me what's going on! I'm not moving until you explain this to me!"

"Merari, I am so sorry but I don't have time right now. We have to get into the ark before God closes the door and sends the rain. If we aren't in before He closes the door, we will die because there will be no way to open the door." Japheth took a deep breath looked up at the sky and spoke in his normal loving voice. "The reason I'm in such a panic is because I thought you had changed your mind and you were not coming. I was on my way to your house to find you and carry you away if I had to. I could not stand the thought of losing you. I could not bear to wait another minute without you. I love you so much and I can't wait for you to become my wife."

I grabbed Japheth's face in my hands. "Japheth, I told

you I was coming. I just had to take care of things at home. I love you, too, and I feel the same urgency as you. I needed some time to say good-bye."

Japheth grabbed me into his arms as if to squeeze away my sadness about leaving my family.

"Come on, let's go. Let's go get married," Japheth said with excitement in his voice.

I wiped away my tears and grabbed Japheth's hand. I once again felt the excitement and anticipation of my new life.

When we reached the ark everything was calm and unlike the scenes it had been in previous days. There were no animals in sight, nor supplies, nor were any of Japheth's family running around.

"Japheth, where is everyone and everything?"

"Everything is in the ark and we have been waiting for you," Noah responded as he came out of the ark. "Japheth run inside and tell everyone to come out so that I can marry you two."

Japheth ran like a child as soon as he heard his father's instructions. Noah gave me a loving hug as everyone came running out of the ark. There were a few minutes of hugging and laughing until Noah said it was time. As I stood there facing Japheth I saw love and caring in his eyes. Every trace of uncertainty and doubt I had disappeared as I looked into Japheth's eyes and heard him promise to be my husband. Then with true love and hope in my new marriage I promised to be his wife.

"Welcome to the family. Let's get into the boat," Noah said laughing.

We kissed for joy. I treasured every second that our lips were together. We would have kissed longer but a loud booming sounded from the sky.

"What's that?" Japheth shouted.

"Quickly get into the ark. We must go now it's about to begin!" Noah shouted.

The terrible sound continued and grew louder and louder. It was so loud that even the ground shook and trembled. I was truly terrified because even though I heard the sound and felt the earth tremble from it, I could not see what was causing it. As soon as we were all in the ark the ramp that our terrified feet had just run over rose up. As the door closed I saw the sky darken as if night was coming. We were all frozen with fright because as we all huddled together the door continued to rise and there was no one pushing it or pulling it. The door rose up and slammed into the side of the ark. There was no denying that God or some supernatural power had closed the door because it slammed shut with such intensity that the entire ark shook and all of the animals fell silent. As soon as the door closed Noah rose up to pray. As I listened to Noah's prayer a sense of peace came over me. Even though my heart seemed to beat out of my chest I realized that I was safe. I was not free from total fear or uncertainty but I knew in my heart that I would be safe and there was a bit of hope and excitement as to what would happen next.

11

A S SOON AS Noah finished his prayer the animals whined and moaned as if in pain or warning each other of danger. It was as if they were questioning why they had been penned up in this huge ark. We were not sure what to think because up until that point the animals appeared to be content in their new surroundings. Each animal, male and female, was penned up in sections of the ark depending on the type and size of the animal. We had all been assigned specific duties and specific animals to care for. Noah suggested that we tour the ark and get to know our surroundings because he was not sure how long we would be in the ark. As we toured Noah explained to each of us our duties and responsibilities. I was truly disgusted when I was told I would help Japheth with the pigs. The pigs smelled terrible. Japheth just smiled and hugged me as if he could read my mind. My other duty was to help my new mother-in-law prepare meals for the family. Noah thought this would be a good experience for me to learn how to cook since he knew I had always had someone prepare my meals.

After the tour Japheth and I went to our small living quarters in the ark. Luckily Noah had given each of us a small private area to use as a bedroom and dressing area. It was nice to finally be alone with Japheth so we could discuss the events of the day.

"Japheth, I'm nervous about this whole thing. I mean it almost feels as if we are trapped in the ark with all kinds of animals and some of these animals eat people." I was glad I could express my concerns to Japheth.

In true Japheth fashion he smiled and said, "Merari, I know you're scared and so am I. What if Dad is wrong and we stay in this ark and it never rains or floods? Who looks like a fool then? We all do. How are we going to explain that to the laughing crowds of people who will be waiting for us when we come out of this ark? The only thing I can do is to have faith that God will fulfill his promise and that He will go through with what He said."

"Wow, Japheth, I didn't know you felt this way," I said.

"I didn't either until we were walking through the ark and it just sort of hit me," Japheth said.

I sat down next to Japheth on our tiny bed and hugged him tightly. "I know one thing and that is that I love you and I would not want to be anywhere else except right here with you." I laughed.

Japheth had a puzzled look on his face and asked, "Why are you laughing?" he asked.

"Well, it appears that I have to be happy here with you because I didn't see any exit doors or windows while we were on the tour." I burst into laughter as Japheth grabbed me around the waist and hugged me.

As we were lying on the bed giggling like two children Noah called to us to come eat. Japheth and I pulled ourselves together and left our tiny room to meet the others for dinner.

At dinner everyone talked about how nervous and excited they were to be in the ark. As the conversations went on my mind drifted back to Mara and my father. I wondered how the engagement party was going, which dress Mara had decided to wear, and what tales my father was embellishing to impress everyone there. As I sat there entangled with my own thoughts the realization of where I was and what I had done sank in. I questioned myself and my decisions, but before I could drown in my self pity and doubt I was shaken back into the conversation by Noah's booming laughter.

"Merari, didn't you get the joke?" Japheth asked.

"Oh, I'm so sorry. My mind was somewhere else. I am sure I would have loved it." I was embarrassed but my new mother-in-law eased my anxiety.

"Japheth, don't give her a hard time. This poor girl has been through a lot these past few days. It is understandable that she's thinking of her family and about what she has gotten herself into. Why, I think Merari is just thinking the same thoughts as all of us. She is just not afraid to explore her fear and doubts," Japheth's mother said reassuringly. "Now let's get this cleaned up and get ready for bed. It has been a long day and I am sure tomorrow will be also because we have to learn to live in this ark and tend to all of these animals."

As we cleaned up dinner my thoughts returned to Mara's engagement party. I wondered what everyone was wearing and who was there. I could not understand why I was having such a difficult time focusing on my new life. Here I was newly married and all I could think about was what I had left behind. As I walked from the eating area back to my tiny room, I felt that nervous feeling in the bottom of my stomach that I used to get as a child when Mara and I would stay with my grandparents for a few weeks. The thoughts of the times Mara and I had spent as children made me smile and brought a small bit of comfort until I realized I would no longer spend my nights with her talking and laughing about the day's events. My feeling of homesickness only increased as wonderful memories filled my mind. As I entered my tiny new room I tried to smile at Japheth, but it was as if he knew what I was thinking.

"I know tonight will be difficult for you because it's your first night away from your family and this is not an ideal place to spend our wedding night. I know you miss your sister and I wish there was some way I could ease your fears," Japheth said lovingly.

I lay down next to Japheth in our bed and he held me tightly in his arms. "The fact that you're trying to understand and help me with my feelings is a great relief. You have no idea how much it helps to know that you understand my fears. I love you so much," I said.

Japheth leaned out of the bed and blew out the tiny glimmering candle. As darkness fell and the sounds of the animals settling into the night filled the room, I closed my eyes and hoped that morning would come quickly.

12

IT SEEMED AS though I had only laid my head down and closed my eyes when suddenly I was awakened by a huge boom. Then the ark shook violently. I sat straight up in bed and clung to Japheth.

"Japheth, what is that?" I cried out.

"I believe God has just fulfilled another promise," Japheth said as he clung to me.

We sat there for what seemed like an hour, but it was only a few minutes. We waited for something else to happen. Japheth fumbled in the darkness to light the candle. Japheth lit the candle to ease our fear. The light of the candle extinguished the blackness of the room. We then heard the pitter patter of something on the roof the ark.

"What's that sound?" I whispered.

"I am not sure," Japheth said as he got out of the bed.

"Where are you going? You aren't going to leave me in here by myself are you?" I was truly terrified.

"No. I am not going to leave you. Come on, let's see if the others hear the same thing. If father's scared then we are in trouble. If anyone knows what is going on he does," Japheth said in a shaky voice.

Japheth grabbed my hand and we walked to the middle of the ark. We found everyone else huddled together around the table where we ate dinner. I was glad we reached the others when we did because all of a sudden the animals wailed, cried, and roared.

As quickly as we had heard the sound of the pitter patter it changed and began to sound as if one hundred waterfalls were crashing over the ark. Then another sound emerged. It was a low rumbling sound. It reminded me mill stones grinding wheat into flour. The sound was like two huge boulders were being rubbed together.

Noah rose to his feet and spoke in a very authoritative voice. "Family, do not be afraid. What we are hearing are the sounds of the fulfillment of God's promise to flood the Earth. He has provided us a safe place to stay and we will not be harmed. I know you're scared, but remember God is faithful. Just remember I have spent the last one hundred years preparing for this moment. God is faithful and He will fulfill his promise to protect us and the animals."

Noah's words were quickly interrupted with shouts and screams from outside the ark pleading for help. We all jumped up from the table and ran to the sides of the ark to hear what the people were saying. It was very difficult to understand many of the screams and cries due to the constant pounding of rain falling on the ark; however, there was one voice I heard clearly. It was Mara's.

"Merari! Merari! Merari!" my sister screamed. "You were right to believe Japheth! I was wrong! I was wrong! Please, let me in! I beg you to help me! I now believe in your God or Japheth's God whoever's God it is just help me! Please!"

My heart and soul ripped in half. I did not know what to do. I knew I had to help her but I also knew there was no way she could get in. In the depth of my soul I realized it was too late for her but I had to try. I desperately looked around for Noah and saw that he was in the middle of the ark walking toward the area where the animals were kept. He must have been going to check on them. I knew that there was no time for him to help because I had to hurry.

"Mara, hang on. I'm going to get help just hang on!" I screamed.

"Merari, is that you? Oh, please, help me!" Mara screamed.

"I am going to get Noah to help me get the door open to let you in!" I screamed back. As soon as the words left my mouth another huge roll of the deafening sound filled the air, the ark suddenly lurched forward then to the side. It was as if the ark was being tossed like a leaf in a strong gusty wind. I fell to the floor and all of the animals cried out.

"Mara! Mara!" I shouted but I was afraid she could not

hear me. I quickly stood up and looked around for Japheth to help. My eyes franticly looked around and then I saw him. He and his brothers were on the top floor of the ark pressing themselves against the small window. It was shut tight just as the door and my mind raced to figure out what they were doing. Suddenly, I realized that they were trying to keep it from being knocked in. I saw them jerk forward as if someone was hitting on it trying to get it open. I could not believe the desperation that was going on. Everyone outside the ark was doing everything they could to save themselves.

"Merari, can you still hear me?" Mara screamed again.

"I am trying, hang on!" I yelled.

"Merari? Merari? Can you hear me? I don't think I can hold on much longer. There are people trying to pull me off this tree because the want my spot!" Mara screamed in a terrified voice.

My mind swirled as I tried to think of a way to help her. I knew that Japheth couldn't because he was trying to keep the window closed so that the water would not rush in and drown all of us. "Mara, I'm trying. I just can't find anybody to help me." I could not believe the helplessness I felt at that moment.

"Merari, ask your God to save me, let me in, open the door, let me pass through the wall of the ark like a ghost, anything. He saved you why can't he save me?"

"Mara, I don't think that will work. I don't know what to do. The only reason I got in is because I believed that God would do what Japheth and Noah said."

"Merari, I need help the water is getting deeper! I don't think I can stand this much longer! The water is up to my knees and the water is rushing by me so fast that I don't think I can hold on to this tree much longer! Merari, just remember that I love you and that you did make the right decision because it is obvious everything I had placed my faith and hope in is about to be washed away."

I could not believe my ears. My sister was giving up. "Mara, don't give up. Hang on. Surely this rain will stop soon. Just hang on and don't give up, please!" My panic became overwhelming because I was afraid she couldn't hear me over the screams and shouts from other people outside of ark. As soon as the words left my lips I heard a great sound of rushing water. Something hit the ark and knocked me down. From the sound and force it must have been a wave of water hitting the ark because it reminded me of the sound of the waves crashing on the beach when we would go to the seashore when I was a child. As I tried to get back up I realized Noah was lying beside me. He grabbed my arm.

"Merari, stay down. It's going to get worse. You'll be safer staying down because the ark is about to be tossed about like a small ship in a storm at sea," Noah said calmly.

"How do you know?" I said sharply. I knew I had to find away to help Mara and lying on the floor was not going to help.

"God said that the oceans would burst forth. There is no way we can stand against the power of the oceans' waves and the flood gates of heaven. We must not try to move until everything has settled down."

I could not believe how calm Noah was. He was so sure. At that moment I agreed with my father that Noah was a nut. I looked around. Everyone else in the ark was crawling toward us. No one looked upset and the animals had calmed down. It was as if the animals were in awe of the sound and the rocking and tossing of the ship. I was apparently the only one having doubts and fears. My doubts and fears quickly vanished because I realized that my sister was gone, swept away by the great waters. Just as I had been tossed about in the safety of the ark she had been swept away with waves so big that they tossed the huge ark like a child's toy boat. I had no desire to lift myself off the floor. All I could do was lay there on the floor of the dry, safe ark, nestled between the members of my new family as my tears dripped from my face and ran through my fingers creating the only puddle on the inside deck of the ark.

13

W E HUDDLED IN the middle of the ark for what seemed like days. Finally the ark stopped being tossed violently, but the sound of the rain continued pounding on the ark. It swayed and rocked like a normal ship in a small storm at sea. The swaying of the ark reminded me of when I was a child. Father often took Mara, mother, and me for trips in his ship. It was great fun and I loved the smell of the ocean and the fresh breeze that continually blew. Those were wonderful, pleasant memories. Noah was the first to stand and speak to us after the frightful events that we had just been through.

"Family, I am glad that we have all survived together and that we have seen that God is faithful and true to his word. He told me that he would send a flood to destroy the earth and due to my faithfulness he would save me and my family. We have now seen his promise come true. Now in his promise he did not say that we would not be scared, frightened, or be able to understand the loss of loved ones and friends. He said He would protect us and He did. I will now say glory to God and thanks to Him for protecting my family. Now, we must try to continue through the rest of this journey. God said he would send rain for forty days and nights and we know that God is faithful and that it will rain for forty days and nights. We have jobs to do and lots of animals to take care of, so let's all head back to our rooms for a short rest and then we'll meet back for a meal. Then we will discuss the plans for the rest of our journey. From my calculations it has been three days since the rain began and I know that we would all need a good night's sleep. So head to your rooms and I will see you all at breakfast in the morning."

I was glad to return to my room to be alone with Japheth. I knew that I needed a good night's sleep because I had not slept since the storm began. All I could do was lie on the floor of the ark and think of my sister and my father being swept away into to waters and that I would never see them again. I prayed that God would allow me the rest I needed to soothe my grief and pain.

When we reached our room Japheth and I both lay down in the bed and held each other tightly. We did not say a word because neither of us knew what to say. Soon we were both fast asleep.

I awoke to the sounds of roosters crowing, cows mooing, and other animal sounds mixed with the sound of the rain.

At first I was disoriented as to where I was. I opened my eyes and found myself staring into the loving eyes of my new husband. After the previous emotional days finally I was able to form a smile as I heard Japheth's sweet voice.

"Good morning, sleepy head. I hope you had a restful night. I am sorry it was not the romantic wedding night that you and I had dreamed of but we are together. I promise you that as soon as we get out of this ark you will have the wedding night you deserve," Japheth said sweetly as he tenderly stroked my hair.

"Japheth, are you kidding? Why did you not realize this is every girl's dream? I mean to spend the wedding night in a huge ship closed up with your in-laws and every possible animal imaginable. Come on this is ideal don't you think?" I laughed. When I regained my composure I noticed Japheth did not find my humor amusing. He just sat there looking at me with a puzzled look on his face.

"Merari, I am glad you can find humor in this situation," he said shortly.

I felt bad because I quickly realized I had hurt his feelings. He was trying to be serious and I was making a joke. "I am sorry Japheth. I was just trying to make the best of this bad, I mean, unusual situation." I was glad I had caught myself before I hurt his feelings any deeper.

"I think I'm having a more difficult time with this than I realized. Maybe today when we get started with our chores and our routines everything will be better."

Japheth was quickly interrupted by the sound of Noah's voice calling everyone to breakfast.

Thought it was morning Japheth had to light the candle so we could dress. The light of the morning sun was not shining because of the rain falling from the sky. The only true way we knew it was morning was from the call of the animals and Noah calling us to breakfast. Japheth and I dressed and walked carefully to eat breakfast with the rest of the family. Before we ate Noah prayed.

"Dear God, thank you for your constant faithfulness and loving kindness. Please, bless this food that we are about to eat. I would also like to thank you for giving me a wonderful family and for providing me with the privilege to travel the journey you have set before me with them. Lord, I humbly ask that you continue daily to strengthen my faith and to allow me to trust you in everything. Lord, again I thank you for your rich blessings. Amen."

After Noah finished praying I looked around the table. They were all beginning to eat and enjoy their meal. It was difficult for me to begin to enjoy the meal because the only light was from the few candles lit on the table. Also the smell of wetness and animals was not very appealing. My mind was also disturbed by Noah's prayer. It appeared that no one but me was disturbed my Noah's prayer. I could not get rid of the uneasy feeling in my stomach as I replayed Noah's prayer in my mind. I could not understand why Noah would ask for a strengthening faith. For crying out loud, he had spent the last one hundred years building a boat because rain was going to fall from the sky and now he was asking for a stronger faith. I was confused. Maybe father was right, maybe Noah was a freak. And here I was stuck in this boat with him. My thoughts were interrupted by Japheth asking me if I would like some more to drink.

"Sure," I said relieved that no one had noticed my doubt or confusion.

As we continued to eat breakfast Noah reviewed everyone's jobs and responsibilities. I was glad to know that for the rest of the day I would be busy and that the day would pass quickly.

The rest of the day passed quickly. After helping my new mother-in-law clear the breakfast dishes and clean up, Japheth and I took care of the pigs. I was surprised to find that I enjoyed my new duties. I had never had such basic responsibilities and it was fun learning how to do so many new things. It was also great fun being with Japheth. We laughed and talked about how we were spending our first day together as man and wife.

At the end of the day as Japheth and I prepared for bed, my mind wandered back to home. Again that sick feeling in my stomach returned and I wanted desperately to be with my father and sister. I did not dare let Japheth in on my feelings. I did not want my yearning for home to ruin the wonderful day we had had together.

Neither I nor Japheth realized how tired we were until

we both laid down in the bed. We gave each other a tender good night kiss and before I had time to tell him goodnight, Japheth was snoring. I closed my eyes hoping that sleep would come to me as quickly, but all that came to me were wonderful memories of home, Mara, father, and of mother. As I lay there in the dark listening to the sounds of the animals and Japheth's snores, cold wet tears trickled down my face. I spent most of the night trying to contain my sobs so I would not shake the bed and wake up Japheth. I wished desperately that I was home again. I also wished that morning would come quickly. Forty days and forty nights without seeing the sun meant enduring greater darkness than I had ever seen before. Darkness and unending rain wore down my spirit.

14

UNFORTUNATELY MORNING came again. I did not
rest well because of an unsettling dream. I dreamt I
was in a small boat, barely large enough to hold me, and I
was headed for a gigantic raging waterfall. The sound of the
waterfall was deafening. The scariest part of the dream was
that even though I was headed for the waterfall, the only
way I could see it was by looking over my left shoulder. If I
looked straight ahead I felt peace and security and I saw a
peaceful pond full of lush greenery, fish, birds, and beautiful
flowers. The boat was heading away from the peaceful pond
and no matter how hard I tried I could not get the boat to
go forward. I had two small oars in the boat with me but no
matter how quickly or strong I rowed the boat was still heading toward the waterfall. I was still shaken and unnerved by
my dream as I got out of bed to dress. The images were so
real that they haunted me. I kept trying to figure out what

the images meant. Did they mean something or was it just my anxiety and nervousness toward my new marriage and living situation?

Japheth must have noticed my anxiety because he asked, "Merari, did you sleep well?"

I was not sure if I should tell him about my dream or just let it go. I decided to tell him. "I had a terrible dream. I keep running the images through my mind trying to make sense them."

"Well, if a dream bothers you maybe you should talk to mother about it. She has a special gift of understanding dreams. Ask her today while you are working together. It will also help pass the time," Japheth said reassuringly.

As we stood there in our bedroom I felt overwhelming love for him. In moments like these my fears and doubts disappeared and I knew I had done the right thing by marrying him. I grabbed him by the arm and he turned to look at me. We drew each other close and shared a loving embrace before we headed off to breakfast.

Everyone ate quickly at breakfast because there was so much work to do. I also think everyone wanted to get to work because it kept our minds off the situation we were in. After everyone finished eating, Noah reminded everyone of their duties and then everyone headed off. Japheth told me he would go ahead and begin our daily chores if I would help his mother clear the table. I knew this was his way of letting me take the time to talk to his mother about my dream.

I helped Japheth's mother clear the table and clean the kitchen area. As we worked I tried to think of a way to bring up my dream without sounding silly. I was nervous about talking with my new mother-in-law. Apparently she sensed my nervousness.

She asked, "Merari would you like to sit and talk for a moment because it appears there is something on your mind."

I was nervous about sharing something so personal but I decided to tell her. "It's very silly but I had a dream and Japheth said you maybe could help explain it." There I had said it and I was waiting for her to laugh or tell me to get back to work but she didn't.

"Merari, I'm so glad you asked for my help. So tell me, what was your dream?"

"I am sitting in a tiny boat and I hear a raging waterfall behind me. In front of me is a beautiful peaceful pond full of lush flowers, birds, fish, and beautiful greenery. Now, this is the scary and strange part of the dream. The boat is heading backwards toward the raging waterfall and no matter how hard I try I can't stop the boat from going backwards and the only way I can see the waterfall is by looking over my shoulder. When I look forward I see the peaceful pond and I want to go there but I can't get the boat to go toward the waterfall." I looked for her reaction. The look on her face was not the reaction I had expected. She smiled at me and her eyes seemed to sparkle. She then got up from where she was sitting, walked over to me, and wrapped her arms around me.

"Oh, Merari, I know why your dream has disturbed you. God is trying to speak to you through this dream."

I could not believe my ears. Now I understand why she married Noah. She was crazy like Noah. "I don't think God is speaking to me," I said.

"Merari, God is trying to show you through a dream about the struggle you are facing and what is in store for you if you turn your faith to him and truly trust in him. I understand your doubt and fear about God because everything you have known all of your life has been washed away. He is trying to show you what He has for you if you can let go of your fear and place your hope and trust in him. The pond is an image of what God provides to those who believe in him. God promises if you believe and trust in him that He will provide for all of your needs. He has even promised that there is a Hope that we can trust in, but that Hope has not yet come, but it will and we must believe in that. The water-fall represents the life that you had before you believed in him. It was uncertain and constantly changing like a water-fall. The boat represents where you are now. You long for the life and hope God has to offer but you also want the life you had before and that is why you can only see it if you look over your shoulder. God is telling you that you must choose one way of life. He wants you to choose Him but the choice is yours. He will not force you to choose Him. All He does is show you what a life is like in his love and protection and the promise of the Hope that is yet to come."

I could not believe my ears. I rudely interrupted her, "What do you mean the Hope that is yet to come?"

"I'm sorry. I didn't mean to upset you," Japheth's mother spoke in a shocked and somewhat embarrassed voice.

I was surprised at my reaction also but I could not help myself. The last words of her sentence were the last words that my mother spoke to me before she died. How did Japheth's mother know this? Why was she saying these things to me? I was in such shock I blurted out, "How could you say that to me and how could you know?"

Confused, Japheth's mother said, "What did I say that has upset you and what am I supposed to know?"

"The Hope that is to come. Those are the last words my mother said to me before she died." I said through my tears as the wound of losing my mother and now having lost my father and sister tore open.

Japheth's mother then held me in her arms as I sobbed uncontrollably. "I had no idea she said that to you. I was only trying to help you understand your dream. It appears that God is trying to help you understand something."

I sat and allowed her to hold me for a long time. I had so many thoughts and questions running through my mind. Why was God talking to me or why would he want to? Why would I have this stupid dream? Why did my family have to die? And why did this thing about hope keep coming up and why did everyone seem to know about it and understand it but me? After a while I pulled myself together, sat back, looked directly in her eyes and asked her to explain this hope to me.

15

ERARI, ARE YOU sure you're ready for this?"

"Please, tell me," I said desperate for answers.

"What I'm about to tell you sounds crazy and I can't explain it thoroughly, all I know is that I believe it. What your mother was telling you is somewhat a mystery and you can only take it by faith. There were only a few people in the world that truly believed the story and they are in this ark."

I was becoming irritated because she seemed to be babbling. "Don't take this the wrong way, but can you get on with the story or whatever it is you have to tell me? I want to know what my mother was trying to tell me. You say it sounds crazy but I'm sitting in a boat with animals and the only people left in the world. What could sound crazier than that?"

"Good point, here goes. Do you remember the story of Adam, Eve and the talking snake?"

I nodded.

"Eve was told by the snake to eat the fruit. She ate it and gave it to Adam and he took a bite. Then God got mad and threw them out of the garden and that's why we're in the mess we are in now."

"Exactly. But there is more to the story than just that. God forced them out of the garden, but he also made a way to rebuild their relationship with him," Japheth's mother said.

"What are you talking about? I don't know many people who have a relationship with God except for you, Noah, and the rest of the family. It seems like you five are the only people in the world who have a relationship with God. I am trying to discover my relationship and belief in God, and with events lately that's beginning to change."

"What do you mean it's beginning to change?" Japheth's mother asked.

I was surprised she asked me this considering what we had just been through. "I think things had to change. Look at where I am and how my life has changed in only a short period of time. I made one simple decision to follow Japheth, believe as he does, and my life has turned upside down. I am living in an ark with animals and the only five people left living on the earth. I have heard the sounds of the most incredible storms ever and I've heard the screams, wails, and cries for help from strangers and my own family. And yet here I am safe, warm, dry, and alive. I constantly ask myself, Why me? Why am I still alive and my family is dead?" At this point I cried as I grieved for my sister, father, and friends.

Japheth's mother took me into her arms and stroked my back as I cried once again for the loss of my family. "I can't explain it all to you, but I know that God has taken care of us for a reason and that reason is because we have believed in Him and His promises."

I cuddled in her arms as she explained the rest of the story to me that my mother was trying to tell me. "Like I said before, God provided a way for Adam and Eve. That's where it gets tricky. In the story God provided clothes for them. To provide the clothing He had to kill an animal to make their clothes and therefore blood was shed. God used the blood of the animal to cover up the sins of Adam and Eve. The covering of their sins enabled their relationship to be restored with God. Now the relationship was restored, but it was not as it once was. Next is the part I don't quite understand, but God made a promise to Adam and Eve that one day the relationship would be restored as it once was but we are not sure how. All we know and have to believe in is that God will someday prepare a different way for us to have an open and holy relationship with him again. This is the Hope that is to come."

I slowly pulled away from her and looked into her eyes. She spoke softly and slowly "Does that answer your questions? I am sure that is what your mother was trying to tell you. Somewhere in your heart you believe in God and his promises or you would not be here with us."

I was not sure what to say but the calming peace I had felt when I decided to leave with Japheth returned. "Yes, I do believe and I know that God will fulfill his promises. You are right and I can't explain it, but after everything I have been through I know there has to be a Hope to come. My mother wanted me to believe and somewhere deep inside I have wanted to believe. I have always felt that there was more to life or a deeper purpose or reason to life. Now I see that God has given me a second chance to find that reason and purpose. I choose to believe in the hope to come." As soon as the words left my lips my heart and spirit lost all the weight, guilt, shame, and uncertainty that I had been feeling. I had to tell Japheth.

"I understand what you're feeling when you discover that there is hope and that it will come. It's as if your inner most being is singing and you have to release its voice or you will explode. Go, tell Japheth."

She was exactly right. It was as if my feet had wings and I could not get to Japheth fast enough. When I found him he was feeding the pigs. I ran and hugged him from behind and said, "I understand! I believe and I know what it means to have hope."

Japheth was shocked with my excitement. He turned to

me and said "I knew you would find what your soul was searching for. Now we can look for the hope together."

We stood there for a long time in each others arms talking about what everything meant and what our lives would now be like living day by day looking for the hope to come. We were brought back to the reality of our situation when the pigs Japheth was feeding grunted and stunk like pigs do have after they have eaten.

16

AFTER I HAD learned of the hope that was to come my perspective on life changed. I no longer looked at life as events that just happen but as events that are shaping me for the greater purpose in life that I have searched for. Even though my perspective on life changed my situation did not. I was still cooped up in an ark with all kinds of animals and with my in-laws and extended family, but my heart and soul sang a different song. It was the song the birds sing after the winter snows have melted and the cold winds have been replaced with the sweet smell of the warm spring breeze. It felt like the morning sunlight shining through the silk curtains into my bed chamber first thing in the morning. I explained this to Japheth's mother and she just smiled and said she understood.

As the days passed it seemed that we were never going to leave the confines of the ark, Japheth and I were leaving our room heading to eat breakfast. We couldn't believe our ears. We stopped and stared at each other in disbelief. The rain had stopped. The continual pounding of the rain on the roof of the ark had stopped. Even the animals were silent. They too had realized the rain had stopped and now there was silence. Japheth and I ran to meet the others at the breakfast table. We all hugged each other and cheered. After all of the time in the ark it might finally be over.

Noah said, "Family, once again God has fulfilled a promise. By my calculations today is the forty-first day and God said it would only rain for forty days and nights. Let's all give a prayer of thanks."

After Noah prayed we all cheered and hugged each other again because soon we would be leaving the ark. Noah then reminded us that until God told us to leave that we all had jobs to do. We all finished eating and got back to our jobs.

The time we had left in the ark was longer than I had anticipated. The days passed slowly because I was ready to leave the ark and spend my time creating my new life as Japheth's wife without all of the animals and the confines of the ark.

One morning as Japheth and I were tending to the pigs the ark jerked and bounced as if it had run into something. Japheth and I were thrown to the ground and all of the animals cried and wailed. Japheth and I scrambled up off the floor and ran to the center of the ark. The rest of the family came running. We eagerly waited for Noah to explain what had just happened.

Noah spoke in an excited tone. "The waters have left the earth and land is starting to appear. What we felt was the ark running aground. I will now send out a raven to see if it is dry and safe enough for us to leave the ark."

As I heard Noah's words my mind raced with excitement that soon, very soon, we would leave the ark. My attention was quickly drawn back to Noah as I heard him say.

"I will wait forty days before I release the raven".

Forty more days. The words repeated over and over in my mind. Forty days, why that's how long it had rained and that seemed like forever. I honestly don't think I can do it I told myself.

"Come on, we need to get back to work," Japheth said.

As Japheth and I went back to our chores I told him my worries. "I don't think I can make it another forty days. I love you and your family but I long for the day when you and I can be our own family and chase our hopes and dreams."

"I know you are weary and so am I but we have to keep our hope and faith that God will see us through these next forty days. He as brought us this far in the adventure. At least we have each other and that is one benefit," Japheth said as he hugged me tightly.

I needed to have his arms around me and to hear his reassuring words. He knew just what to say to help me deal with my worries. Deep in my heart I knew he was right and I knew I could depend on God.

The next forty days crept by. We all went about our daily chores and activities but everyone was ready to leave the ark. The animals sensed our anticipation because their cries and sounds had a desperate sound to them.

Finally on the forty-first day Noah climbed to the level of the ark where there was a window. He slowly opened the window. As the window slowly opened the sunlight came shining in as a rushing wind. We all had to close our eyes because the light was so bright. My skin tingled as the light and the warmth from the sun hit my skin. All the animals sent out sounds of excitement as the sunlight penetrated every corner and crevasse of the ark. Through squinted eyes I watched as Noah lifted the raven and sent him out of the ark.

After Noah released the raven he turned to us and said, "The raven will fly over the earth until all the water has dried up. We will again have to patiently wait to see what the raven discovers."

I didn't care how long it took that bird to find dry land. I knew the end of our time in the ark was near.

For another forty days the raven flew over the earth. No one seemed to mind because Noah left the window open and the sunlight and fresh air lifted everyone's spirits. The air smelled fresh and greatly helped the smells inside the ark improve.

One morning as Japheth and I were finishing our chores, we noticed Noah standing at the window with a bird but it wasn't the raven.

"Dad," Japheth said. "What are you doing and why do you have a different bird"?

"It is now time for me to send out a dove. I will now send a dove to look for dry land and plants," Noah answered.

Japheth and I looked at each other with excitement. We rushed back to our chores as if our rushing would hurry the bird and its findings.

Every evening at dinner everyone asked Noah if the dove had returned with the proof he needed to leave the ark. After Noah told us all "no" we would discuss our plans for when we left the ark.

One day we were all gathering for the midday meal when Noah came running toward us. He was so excited we could barely understand what he was trying to say.

"An olive leaf! An olive leaf! The dove has returned with an olive leaf! This is a sign that all the water has receded and plant life has begun again!"

Japheth spoke first, "Father are you sure? What will it be like when we leave? We are the only six people left on the earth. What will we do?"

I was glad Japheth asked because I was thinking the same thing.

Noah spoke. "If God has brought us this far He will lead us the rest of the way. We have no room to doubt because

He has always been faithful and now we must be faithful to obey and trust Him."

I could not believe what happened next but out of my mouth came the words, "Yes, we must believe and look for the Hope that is to come as we walk through the doors of the ark and into this new world."

I think everyone was surprised at what I said. The words I had spoken were suddenly forgotten because the door of the ark fell open and sunlight flooded through the door and into the ark. No one moved because even though we had adjusted to the small amount of sun light from the small window we were blinded by the sunlight. At that moment the cages that had held the animals fell open and the animals raced out into the sunlight. The ark shook and trembled with the movement of the animals leaving.

Noah was the first to step onto the ramp which had once been the door that had held us safely tight for so long. I saw sunlight shining off of his head and it was all most blinding. We followed Noah into the sunlight. As I stepped out I quickly had to cover and shield my eyes due to the bright sunshine. It took several minutes for my eyes to adjust. As I opened my eyes I could hardly believe them. Everywhere I looked there was new life. The trees were green, the grass was green. High mountains around us were covered with beautiful flowers. The flowers were incredible. The flowers and grass covered the ground like colorful rugs. Other plants and trees grew tall as if saluting the sun. Even with all of the beauty around me the most distinguishing thing about this place was the smell, the smell of freshness. It was as if every breath drew in new life and freshness and every exhale removed the stale air from my old life.

Noah said, "Family, today is another day that fulfills a promise God has made to us. As you can see, smell, and feel, God has delivered us from the terrible storm and has provided us a place of beauty in which to live. We must always be thankful for this and treasure the gifts God has given us. As you see He has brought life back into this world. Life that is beautiful and fresh. Look at the animals. They are stretching, running, playing, and exploring this new world God has given them. We must do the same. We must always remember what God has done for us. Now, let us pray, worship, and thank God for his safety, deliverance, and new opportunity at life."

As I listened to Noah's prayer I prayed in my own heart a prayer of thanksgiving, worship, and a prayer requesting help. I was thankful for Japheth, my new family, and for being alive in this wonderful new place. I worshipped God for saving me from the terrible flood, for the opportunity to experience his greatness and caring love. But then I prayed for help to continue strengthening my faith in my journey to know Him more. I prayed for help to overcome the sadness over losing my family. I also prayed for help to be the wife I needed to be to Japheth. As I finished my prayer I felt so overwhelmed to know that I had a God who understood how I could praise him for all of the wonderful things He has done and who also understands my weaknesses and frailties. What a great God who understands all, knows all, and loves all.

After our time of prayer Noah led the family in preparing a meal of celebration. It was wonderful being able to celebrate and experience a party again. We all laughed, sang, danced, and shared funny stories and memories of things that had happened over the past months. Before we ate our evening meal we all noticed an incredible sight in the bright blue sky. It was an arch of color that stretched across the sky. The colors were red, orange, yellow, green, light blue, dark blue, and purple. We all stood there in awe of the beautiful sight.

"What you see is a sign from God declaring his promise that He will never flood the earth again," Noah explained.

Noah said another prayer thanking God for always keeping his promises and protecting us. After we ate we again shared all the things we were thankful for. As evening came we all went back into the ark because we had no shelter until we could build and begin to create a new community. Everyone said good night.

When we returned to our room I noticed Japheth was quiet. I sat done beside him on the bed with my arm rubbing his back and my head pressed on his shoulder. "Japheth, are you well?" I asked.

He turned toward me and held my other hand. "What

a day it's been. This morning we were still closed up in this ark and this afternoon we walked on dry ground, saw trees and flowers, and smelled fresh air again. I'm in awe of what God has done for us. I'm also in awe of what He still has planned for us. I wonder what else he has in store for us. It's exciting and frightening at the same time."

We sat on the edge of the bed and hugged each other for a long time because words could not express the span of emotions we both were feeling. After a while Japheth sat back and asked, "Are you scared about our future?"

With assurance I answered, "No. I'm not scared because over the past months I've learned so much about God and I know that He will provide a way. I know with assurance that He provides hope and that there is hope coming. When we began this adventure I didn't know a thing about God except that you and your family believed in Him. That was all I needed because I loved you and wanted to be with you. And if that meant believing in your God then I did it. But now He's my God. He saved me from this awful storm, provided me with a loving family, and an opportunity to start a new life." As I finished my answer my heart filled with joy, excitement, and assurance that I had a future and it was future worth looking forward to.

"I didn't know you felt that way. I guess we both still have a lot to learn about God and each other."

"Yes, we do, but you know the best part?"

"What's that?"

"The best part is that we get to do it together without being stuck on a boat with a bunch of smelly animals."

"You're right about that," Japheth laughed.

We laughed and talked for hours. It was fun to laugh and talk with my husband again. The daily stresses of living and working on the ark had taken their toll on us. Even though we knew that we had a great task before us we knew that with the hope God would provide we could do it together.